I am a very Clever Cat

Kasia Matyjaszek

templar publishing

Hello! My name is Stockton.
I am a **very** clever cat.

Look what I can **do** . . .

I am just **SO** smart.

But what I do best is . . .

. . . knitting!

Knitting is nothing for a **talented** cat like me.

Watch me knit the fanciest scarf for the fanciest soirée.

Bright pink will be **perfect**.

And casting on . . . .

. . . is **easy!**

Who needs a pattern?

I make it up as I go along.

A stitch here . . .

. . . a loop there . . .

. . . and a **big** knot
or two.

This is going to be the **best** scarf **ever!**

And now for the finishing touches . . .

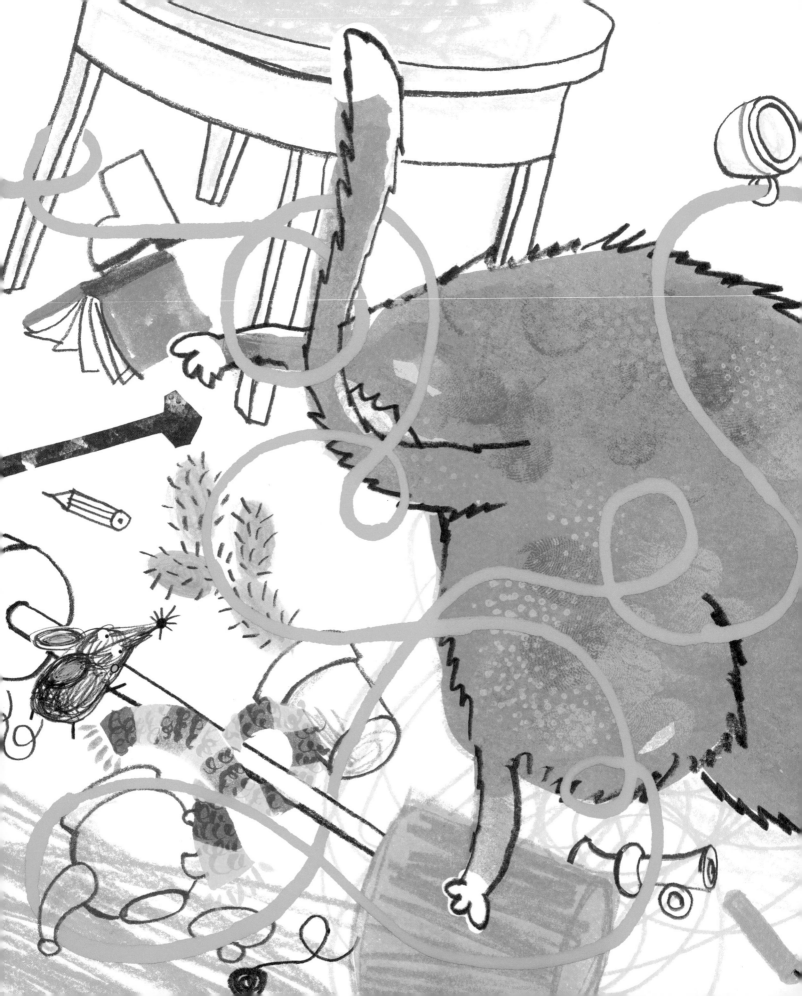

Oh dear. Look what I've done.

Now I'll **never** go to the fancy soirée.

But wait, what's this . . . ?

My name is Stockton
and I am a very **smart** cat . . .

. . . with some very **clever** friends.